W9-COB-619

FOX

MARGARET WILD
and Ron Brooks

KANE/MILLER
BOOK PUBLISHERS

First American Edition 2001 by Kane/Miller Book Publishers
La Jolla, California

Originally published in Australia in 2000 by Allen & Unwin
Text copyright © Margaret Wild 2000
Illustrations copyright © Ron Brooks 2000

All rights reserved. For information contact:
Kane/Miller Book Publishers
P.O. Box 8515
La Jolla, CA 92038-8515
Library of Congress Cataloging-in-Publication Data

Wild, Margaret, 1948-
Fox/Margaret Wild and Ron Brooks [illustrator]. - American ed. p. cm.
Summary: An injured magpie and a one-eyed dog live happily together in the forest,
until a jealous fox arrives to teach them what it means to be alone.
ISBN 1-929132-16-6
[1.Friendship-Fiction. 2.Magpies-Fiction. 3.Dogs-Fiction. 4.Foxes-Fiction.]I.Brooks, Ron,
ill. II.Title
PZ7W64574Fo 2001   [E]-dc21   2001029573

Book design by Ron Brooks. Artwork is mixed media and collage.
The text of this book was hand-lettered by Ron Brooks.

Printed and bound in Singapore by Tien Wah Press Pte. Ltd.

1 2 3 4 5 6 7 8 9 10

For Ron, Rosalind and Sarah,
With thanks. M.W.

To M.W. for the words
and to Margaret, for the waiting. R.B.

THROUGH THE CHARRED FOREST, over hot ash, runs Dog, with a bird clamped in his big, gentle mouth. He takes her to his cave above the river, and there he tries to tend her burnt wing;

but Magpie does not want his help.

"I will never again be able to fly," she whispers.

"I know," says Dog. He is silent for a moment, then he says, "I am blind in one eye, but life is still good."

"An eye is nothing!" says Magpie. "How would you feel if you couldn't run?"

Dog does not answer. Magpie drags her body into the shadow of the rocks, until she feels herself melting into blackness.

DAYS, perhaps a week later, she wakes with a rush of grief. Dog is waiting. He persuades her to go with him to the riverbank.

"Hop on my back," he says. "Look into the water and tell me what you see."

Sighing. Magpie does as he asks. Reflected in the water are clouds and sky and trees — and something else.

"I see a strange new creature," she says. "That is us," says Dog. "Now hold on tight!"

With Magpie clinging to his back, he races through the scrub, past the stringybarks, past the clumps of yellow box trees, and into blueness. He runs so swiftly. it is almost as if he were flying.

Magpie feels the wind streaming through her feathers, and she rejoices. "FLY, DOG, FLY! I will be your missing eye, and you will be my wings."

And so Dog runs, with Magpie on his back, every day, through Summer, through Winter.

After the rains,
when saplings are
  springing up everywhere,
a fox comes into the bush;
Fox with his haunted eyes
  and rich red coat.
He flickers through the trees
like a tongue of fire,
and Magpie trembles.

"Thank you," says Fox. "I saw you running this morning. You looked extraordinary."

Dog beams, but Magpie shrinks away.

She can feel Fox staring at her burnt wing.

In the evenings, when the air is creamy with blossom,
Dog and Magpie relax at the mouth of the cave,
enjoying each other's company.
Now and again Fox joins in the conversation,
but Magpie can feel him watching,
always watching her.

And at night his smell seems to fill the cave—
a smell of rage and envy and loneliness.

Magpie tries to warn Dog about Fox.
"He belongs nowhere," she says. "He loves no one."
But Dog says, "He's all right. Let him be."

That night, when Dog is asleep, Fox whispers to Magpie,
"I can run faster than Dog. Faster than the wind.
  Leave Dog and come with me."
  Magpie says, "I will never leave Dog. I am his
missing eye and he is my wings."

Again Magpie says, "I will never leave Dog. I am his missing eye and he is my wings."

But later that day, as Dog runs through the scrub with Magpie on his back, she thinks, "This is nothing like flying. Nothing!"

Fox says no more that night, but the next day when Dog is at the river, he whispers to Magpie, "Do you remember what it is like to fly? Truly fly?"

And when at dawn Fox whispers to her for the third time, she whispers back, "I am ready."

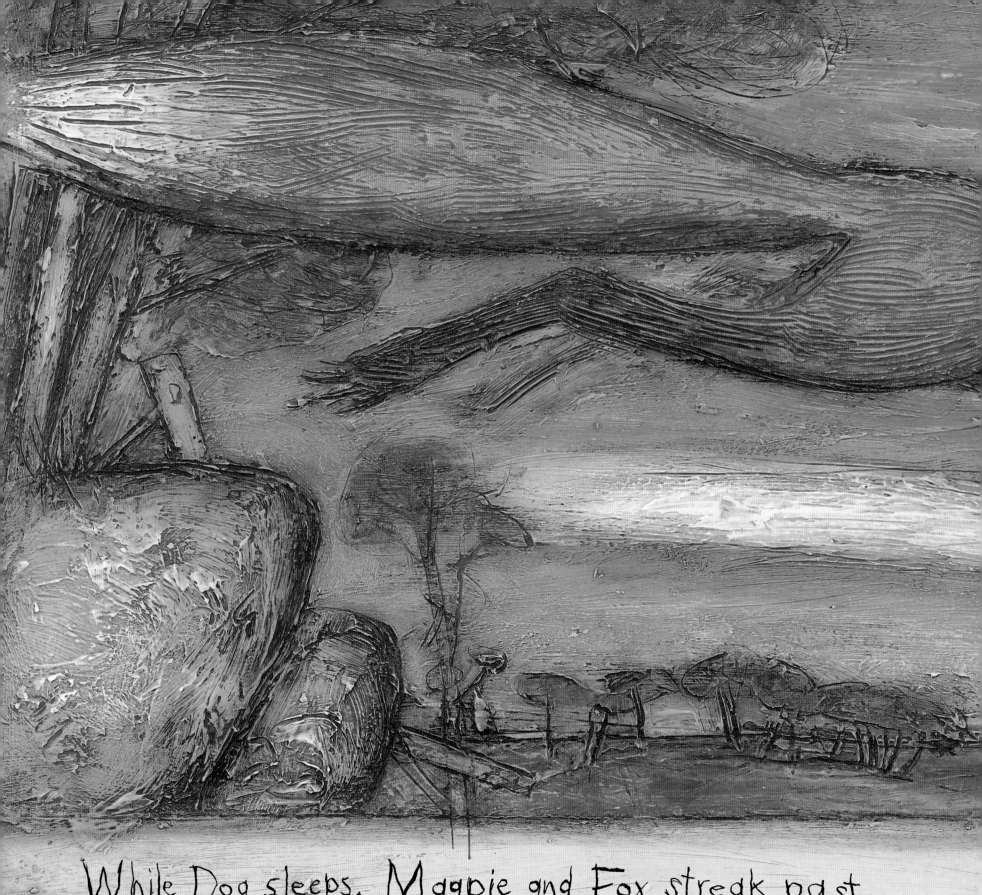

While Dog sleeps, Magpie and Fox streak past coolibah trees, rip through long grass, pelt over rocks.

Fox runs so fast that his feet scarcely touch the ground, and Magpie exults, "At last I am flying, Really Flying!"

Fox scorches through woodlands, through dusty plains, through salt pans, and out into the hot red desert.

He stops, scarcely panting.
there is silence between them.
Neither moves, neither speaks.

Then Fox shakes Magpie off his back
as he would a flea,
and pads away.

He turns and looks at Magpie, and he says,
"Now you and Dog will know what it is like
to be truly alone."
Then he is gone.
In the stillness, Magpie hears a faraway scream.
She cannot tell if it is a scream of triumph
or despair.

Magpie huddles, a scruff of feathers adrift in heat.
She can feel herself burning into nothingness.
It would be so easy just to die here in the desert.

But then she thinks of Dog waking to find her gone.

Slowly, jiggety-hop,
she begins the long journey home.